SCOOTER BINGHAM
and the LITTLE DUCKLING

PAGE PUBLISHING, INC.
New York, NY

First originally published by Page Publishing, Inc. 2017

ISBN 978-1-68409-344-1 (Paperback)
ISBN 978-1-68409-345-8 (Digital)

Printed in the United States of America

SCOOTER BINGHAM
and the LITTLE DUCKLING

Alexander McRae "Rooster" Beebe

SEPTEMBER 26, 2018
GIVEN TO ST. PAUL'S EPISCOPAL SCHOOL

IN LOVING MEMORY OF

JOHN McRAE (JACK) BEEBE
RECTOR ST PAUL'S CHURCH
1980-1992

Meet Scooter Bingham

Scooter Bingham is a cowboy who
works the Branded B.
He started at the age of eighteen and now is twenty-three.

He tips the scale at one-fifteen, five from worn out boots.
His legs resemble willow twigs that bow like
dried up roots.

His curly hair is auburn red, his ears are rather large.
His eyes appear a forest green, his skin is freckled and his frame is lean.

His silhouette sparks amusement from the cowboys all around.
When the sun would rise and fall he'd cast the letter **C** against the ground.

Scooter doesn't mind the ribbing he often takes.
He feels great pride in how he looks and the shadows that he makes.

Scooter Bingham's day starts at 5:00 a.m.
when the rooster sings his song.
He washes his face, combs his hair, and grabs his boots—the dusty pair.

A biscuit and some bacon fill his tiny frame.
Then off he runs to do his chores and live the cowboy's dream.

Scooter loves to ride his pony around the Branded B,
a frisky paint named Applejack who loves to run and play.

Together they roam the ranch working side by side:
riding fences, chasing strays, feeding cattle, and bailing hay.

Scooter loves the cowboy life and the freedom that he feels.
He wouldn't trade a single day for doing something else.

When darkness comes he hangs his hat and pulls his dusty boots.
He smiles at his reflection in the mirror in his room.

He's not your average cowboy that works the Branded B.
But Scooter Bingham loves his life and that is plain to see.

So now you've met young Scooter Bingham
and he'd love if you'd tag along
and share in his adventures that last the whole day long.

And when the day is over and it's time to go to sleep,
dream of great adventures Scooter Bingham and you will meet.

On a cold and windy day, Scooter
Bingham is out in the barn
stacking hay. Stacking hay is not one
of Scooter's favorite jobs, but he does
it with a great attitude knowing that
the job needs to be done, and he
always takes great pride in his work.

"If a job's worth doing, it's worth doing right," says Scooter.

Scooter Bingham's horse, Applejack, is just outside the barn waiting
for Scooter to finish so they can move onto their next chore. Applejack is
always with Scooter Bingham, and they love each other very much.

Before long, Scooter Bingham comes out and finds Applejack trying to comfort a duckling that appears to be lost. Scooter can tell the duckling is cold and lonely and needs their help. Scooter has a special gift for always being kind and gentle. All the animals on the ranch love Scooter very much.

5

Scooter bends down and rubs the duckling on his head and says, "It will be alright, little fella. Applejack and I will help you get back home." Scooter then wraps him in an old feed sack that was in the barn and places him in one of Applejack's saddlebags. Scooter tells the duckling, "Now that we have met and are no longer strangers I need to give you a name. I think I will call you Rascal." Applejack nods with approval and off they ride to find Rascal's home. Scooter and Applejack are very familiar with the Branded B. The two of them had traveled every fence line all around the ranch.

Scooter tells Applejack, "Let's
start by looking near the south pond.
Ducks love water, and I'm sure that's
where we will find Rascal's family."

Applejack knows the way, and
off they go. Scooter and Applejack
look back at Rascal secure in the
saddlebag, and they can tell he is safe,
warm, and happy to be going home.

Little did the three of them
know that their day was about to
turn into a great adventure!

About an hour later the three of them arrive at the south pond. Scooter takes Rascal out of the warm saddlebag and places him on the ground. "Does any of this look familiar?" Scooter asks Rascal.

Rascal looks around for a while, but he doesn't seem to know where he is.

Scooter walks over near the pond to see if he can find Rascal's family. Ducks usually hang around water. Scooter is surprised that there are no ducks in the pond. "Well don't get discouraged, Rascal. We'll find your home very soon."

Scooter then places Rascal back in the saddlebag and tells Applejack, "Let's try the west pond. I'm sure we'll find Rascal's family there."

Applejack heads off to the west pond which is about an hour away.

Along the way Scooter Bingham starts thinking about all his chores that will not get done today. He also remembers he forgot to tell anyone where he was going or how long he would be gone. "Oh well," Scooter thought to himself, "we should be back before anyone notices."

Around noon Scooter, Applejack, and Rascal arrive at the west pond. "I'm sure this must be the place," says Scooter as he places Rascal back on the ground. Rascal runs over to the water's edge and jumps in the pond. "I guess this must be it," says Scooter.

But soon Rascal comes out of the water with a sad look on his face. Scooter can tell that Rascal was not able to find his family, and Rascal is very sad.

Although Scooter knows of one more pond on the ranch, he is getting concerned about finding Rascal's family. The last pond is the farthest away and will take several hours to get there.

"I guess we better get going," says Scooter. Scooter can see the worried look in Applejack's eyes, but Scooter assures him, too, that everything will be all right.

"I don't want either of you to worry about anything. We will find Rascal's home if it takes us all day."

So off the three of them go to continue their search for Rascal's family.

Along the way they stop at an old Live Oak Tree where Scooter says, "I think this will be a great place to have lunch."

As always Scooter has packed a lunch and placed it in one of Applejack's saddlebags. There is always an extra apple in his lunch for Applejack.

Scooter tells Rascal, "That's why I call him Applejack. He loves apples!" Scooter smiles at Rascal and gives him a piece of his sandwich. After everyone has rested and eaten their lunch they continue their journey to the last pond on the ranch.

After a long two-hour ride the trio finally arrives at the last pond. Scooter sees the excitement on Rascal's face.

"I guess this must be the place," says Scooter. Rascal starts jumping around with excitement and anticipation ready to be reunited with his family.

"He obviously recognizes this pond," Scooter says to Applejack.

Applejack stomps his hoof with excitement. Rascal runs immediately to a nest near the pond's edge. Scooter can tell a duck family lives there, but Rascal and Scooter did not find anyone home. Rascal jumps in the water quacking and quacking in search of his family, but no one answers.

Scooter looks back at Applejack. They each have a worried look on their face because it is getting late, and it won't be too much longer before it starts getting dark.

Scooter wraps up Rascal in the feed sack and tells him, "I am so sorry we did not find your family, Rascal, but it is getting late, and we need to start heading back to the bunkhouse. We will continue our search tomorrow if necessary." Rascal looks very discouraged but knows they need to go back.

On the trail home Scooter comes across some animal tracks that he recognizes, and he becomes very concerned. Although Scooter is loved by all the ranch animals there is one animal Scooter and Applejack always try to avoid. Scooter knows these tracks belonged to a ferocious mountain lion that has only been seen on the Branded B a few times. Applejack and Scooter proceed very cautiously down the trail. It isn't long before the mountain lion tracks disappear into the brush, and Scooter exhales with relief.

Suddenly, and without any
warning, Scooter, Applejack, and
Rascal hear a loud growl coming from
the brush and on the trail just behind
them is the mountain lion making his
way down the trail toward them.

Now there's one thing Scooter knows about Applejack that Rascal doesn't know. Applejack is the fastest pony on the Branded B and has never lost a race to any of the other ponies. Scooter yells, "Make like the wind, Applejack!" And Applejack takes off like a rocket down the trail.

Although the mountain lion takes off chasing them, it isn't long before the cat gives up the chase and watches the dust made by Applejack's rapidly clicking hooves.

"I think we lost him," says Scooter to Applejack. Applejack stops and turns around and raises up on his hind legs with a loud neigh! Scooter, Applejack, and Rascal can see the mountain lion heading over the hills far away from them.

"Well that was way too much excitement for one day," says Scooter. Applejack neighs again and stomps his hoof in agreement then they continue their journey back to the bunkhouse.

As the sun starts to set Scooter can see the bunkhouse in the distance.

"We are almost home," says Scooter to Applejack and Rascal. Scooter is wondering why Rascal's family is no longer at the pond and where they should look tomorrow. Although Scooter is concerned, he doesn't let Rascal know.

When they arrive at the bunkhouse Applejack walks into the
barn where Scooter keeps his saddle. Scooter takes Rascal out of
the saddlebag and places him on some warm hay. "You can sleep
here tonight, Rascal. The hay will keep you warm and safe."
As Scooter is removing Applejack's saddle he hears
what sounds like a quack coming from outside.

Scooter and Rascal walk out of
the barn and then hear several more quacks
coming from Applejack's water trough.
There, swimming in the trough is Rascal's
family. Apparently Rascal's family went looking
for him at the same time Rascal, Scooter and
Applejack went looking for Rascal's family.
At least they all ended up at the same place at the end of the day!
    Scooter invites all of Rascal's family to spend the night in
the barn where they will be warm and safe for the night.

Scooter brushes Applejack, feeds him some oats, and thanks him for being such a great horse and best friend. Applejack rubs his face against Scooter's cheek and walks into his stall.

Scooter ambles into the bunkhouse and smiles at his reflection in the mirror.

"I'm not your average cowboy," Scooter thinks with pride as he pulls off his boots, hangs his hat and spurs, washes his face, and lays his head down on his pillow, giving thanks for having such a great cowboy life. As Scooter falls asleep, he wonders what great adventure awaits him tomorrow.

About the Author

Alexander McRae "Rooster" Beebe

Rooster is a doting and engaged grandfather who has the uncanny knack of capturing life's ordinary and often under-observed experiences and penning them into poignant, tender moments.

He is known for his adventurous spirit. At the age of four, while living in Italy, he pedaled his sleek red Giordani Ferrari style sports car several blocks away to the city park unbeknownst to his family. AND, thus the adventures of his imagination were born. From Tarzan adventures in the "jungle" behind his home in Pittsburgh, to cowboy exploits across the great state of Texas, Rooster was born for adventure. He truly has a love for all things cowboy and the Wild West.

He first created Scooter as a secondary character in a short story. However, Scooter's charm, ten-gallon hat personality, and altogether good looks immediately took life in Rooster's imagination, and Scooter Bingham and the Little Duckling is the first in a series of delightful adventures.

Rooster enjoys spending time with family, long walks in the country, gardening, scuba diving, all things beach, and playing the guitar. Bits and pieces from these experiences meld with Rooster's imagination and often show up as events in Scooter's all but ordinary life on the Branded B.

He resides in Boerne, Texas located in the Texas Hill Country where he lives with his lovely and talented wife Pattie. They have five beautiful daughters, four extraordinary grandchildren (who call him Rooster), a rascally dog named Tucker, and a cantankerous, yet loving cat they call Tobias.

CPSIA information can be obtained
at www.ICGtesting.com
Printed in the USA
LVHW07s1301290818
588512LV00023B/454/P